SAMMY SPIDER'S
NEW
FRIEND

This
PJ BOOK
belongs to

_____

_____

Pj Library®

JEWISH BEDTIME STORIES and SONGS

Sylvia A. Rouss

Illustrated by
Katherine Janus Kahn

KAR-BEN
PUBLISHING

To all my friends & family. I treasure their love and support. —S.A.R.

*To Madeline, whose glowing watercolors are an inspiration,
and who believed in Sammy from the beginning.* —K.J.K.

*In Memory of Nancy Kaplan, who was the voice and heart of customer
service at Kar-Ben, and whose warmth and generosity will be missed.*
—Kar-Ben Publishing.

Text copyright © 2012 by Sylvia A. Rouss
Illustrations copyright © 2012 by Katherine Janus Kahn

KAR-BEN PUBLISHING
A division of Lerner Publishing Group, Inc.
241 First Avenue North
Minneapolis, MN 55401 U.S.A.
1-800-4-Karben

Website address: www.karben.com

Library of Congress Cataloging-in-Publication Data

Rouss, Sylvia A.
  Sammy Spider's new friend / by Sylvia A. Rouss ; illustrated by
Katherine Janus Kahn.
    p.   cm.
  Summary: As the Shapiros prepare to welcome a new family
to their neighborhood, Sammy, a young spider who lives in the
Shapiro's house, is blown by the wind into the neighbor's yard
and entertains little Moti, who speaks to him in Hebrew.
  ISBN 978–0–7613–6663–8 (lib. bdg. : alk. paper)
  [1. Friendship—Fiction. 2. Spiders—Fiction. 3. Moving,
Household—Fiction. 4. Jews—United States—Fiction.] I. Kahn,
Katherine, ill. II. Title.
PZ7.R7622Sag 2012
[E]—dc23   2011029755

Manufactured in the United States of America
1 – BP – 2/2/13

Sammy Spider dangled from his web next to an
open window in the Shapiros' kitchen.

Josh was helping
Mrs. Shapiro mix
batter in a bowl.

"What are they doing?"
Sammy called to his mother,
who was busy spinning a web
on the ceiling.

"They are making a cake for the new family moving in next door," answered Mrs. Spider.

Sammy listened. "When the cake is done," Mrs. Shapiro told Josh, "we'll take it over to welcome our new neighbors who have just moved here from Israel."

"Can we bake a cake, too?" Sammy asked his mother.

"Silly little Sammy," she answered. "Spiders don't bake cakes. Spiders spin webs."

Just then, Mr. Shapiro came into the kitchen. "Should we also bring a loaf of bread and some salt?" he asked. "It's a Jewish custom to bring these when someone moves into a new home," he explained to Josh. "It is our wish that they enjoy many happy meals together."

"Why don't we bring pita and hummus?" suggested Josh. "Pita is Israeli bread and hummus is a salty dip."

"What a great idea!" said his dad.

Sammy wished he could welcome the new neighbors, too. He gazed out the window and watched men unloading boxes from a large truck.

Suddenly, a breeze snapped a strand of
webbing and carried the little spider high
into the air.

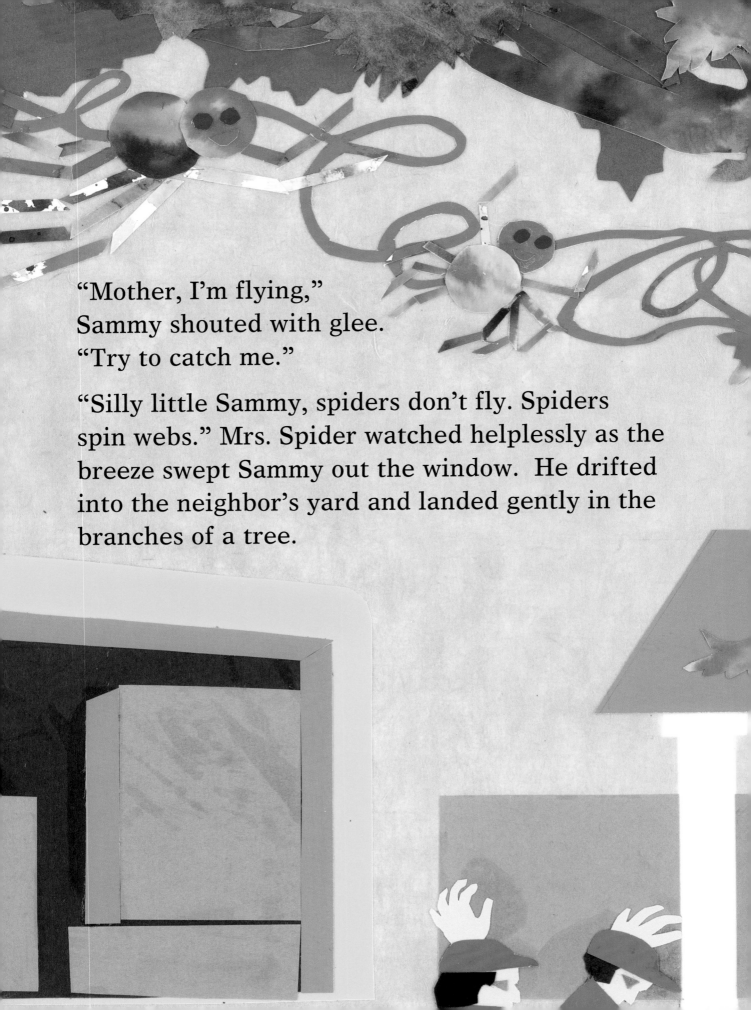

"Mother, I'm flying,"
Sammy shouted with glee.
"Try to catch me."

"Silly little Sammy, spiders don't fly. Spiders spin webs." Mrs. Spider watched helplessly as the breeze swept Sammy out the window. He drifted into the neighbor's yard and landed gently in the branches of a tree.

"Come back when the wind calms down," she called to him.

Sammy heard
someone crying.

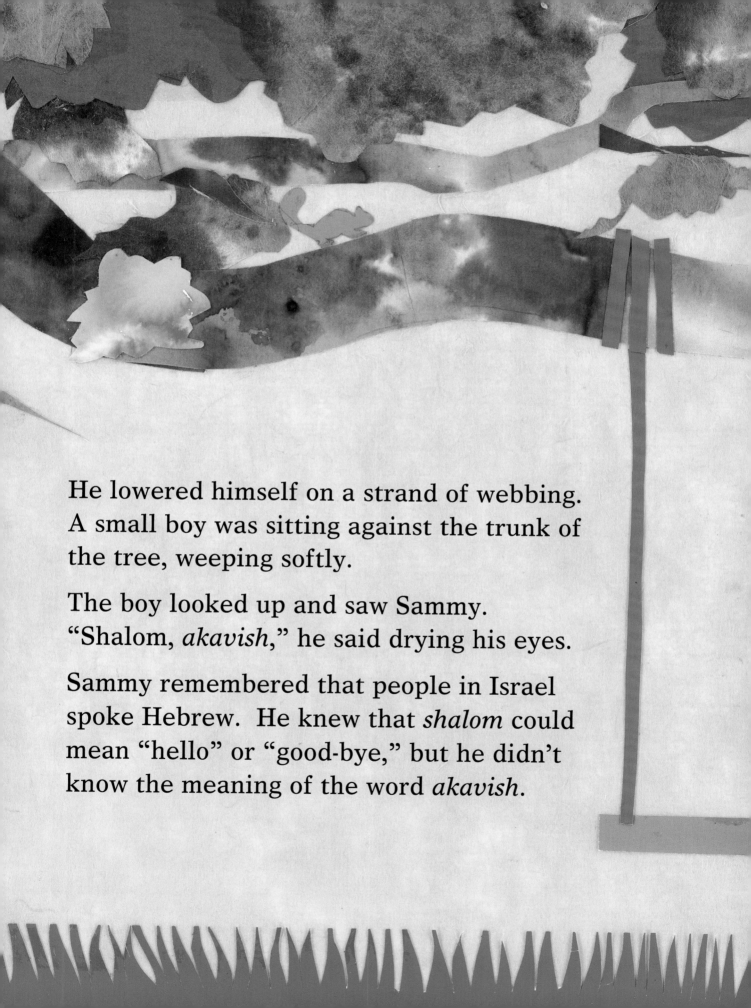

He lowered himself on a strand of webbing. A small boy was sitting against the trunk of the tree, weeping softly.

The boy looked up and saw Sammy. "Shalom, *akavish*," he said drying his eyes.

Sammy remembered that people in Israel spoke Hebrew. He knew that *shalom* could mean "hello" or "good-bye," but he didn't know the meaning of the word *akavish*.

The boy seemed so sad that Sammy decided to spin a web to cheer him up. He spun faster and faster and soon the little boy began to smile.

"I've made a new friend," thought Sammy. "And he looks happy to have a new friend, too."

As Sammy finished his web, he saw the
Shapiros come up the walkway. Mrs.
Shapiro was carrying a cake, Mr. Shapiro
was carrying pita and hummus, and Josh
was carrying a blanket, a bat, and a ball.

When the little boy saw the
visitors, he ran inside to get
his mother and father.

The families introduced themselves. The little boy, whose name was Moti, helped Josh spread the blanket under the tree.

Everyone sat down to enjoy the food
and to get to know each other.

Afterwards, Sammy watched Josh and Moti play ball. Then they took turns on the big tree swing, and when they got tired, they settled down to a game of checkers.

Sammy was happy to see Josh and Moti laughing and having fun together.

When the Shapiros got ready to leave, Sammy waited as Josh folded the blanket and tossed it over his shoulder. The little spider climbed on to catch a ride home.

Good-bye friend

Moti turned to Josh. "Shalom, *haver*," he said
in Hebrew, and Josh responded in English,
"Good-bye, friend."

Then Moti smiled up at Sammy and winked, "Shalom, *akavish*."

"I guess *haver* means friend, but what does *akavish* mean?" Sammy wondered as he snuggled into the blanket.

שלום עכשיו

Mrs. Spider was waiting in her web when Sammy returned. "Mother, I made a new friend today. His name is Moti and he speaks Hebrew. I watched him play ball with Josh. And when I left, he said, '*Shalom, akavish.*' I know what *shalom* means, but I don't know the word *akavish*. Maybe I can find out the next time I see him. Can I play ball with him tomorrow?"

"Silly little Sammy," laughed Mrs. Spider. "An *akavish* doesn't play ball. An *akavish* spins webs!"

THE JEWISH CUSTOM OF HOSPITALITY
dates back to the time of Abraham and Sarah,
who invited three strangers into their tent and
provided them with food and shelter. Sammy
learns about this important mitzvah as he watches
the Shapiro family welcome their new neighbors.

HEBREW WORDS

Shalom: hello, good-bye, peace

Haver (ha-vair, "h" pronounced like the "ch" in "Bach"): friend

Akavish (ah-ka-veesh): spider

HUMMUS

1 16-oz. can garbanzo beans (reserve liquid)
1/8 cup liquid (from the beans)
1 clove garlic, crushed
1 Tbsp. olive oil
1/2 Tbsp. water
1/2 tsp. salt
lemon juice to taste (2-4 tsps.)
2 Tbsp. tahini (sesame paste)

Drain beans and set aside liquid. Combine remaining ingredients in blender or food processor. Blend on low until thoroughly mixed and smooth. Additional lemon juice or garbanzo bean liquid may be added to achieve desired consistency.

Recipe courtesy Evie Sabes, Louisville, Kentucky